Cinderella

First published in 2001 by
Franklin Watts
96 Leonard Street
London
EC2A 4XD

Franklin Watts Australia
56 O'Riordan Street
Alexandria
NSW 2015

A CIP catalogue record for this book is available
from the British Library.

ISBN 0 7496 4045 6 (hbk)
ISBN 0 7496 4228 9 (pbk)

Series Editor: Louise John
Series Advisor: Dr Barrie Wade
Series Designer: Jason Anscomb

Printed in Hong Kong

Cinderella

by Barrie Wade

Illustrated by Julie Monks

W
FRANKLIN WATTS
LONDON•SYDNEY

Once upon a time there was a beautiful young girl called Cinderella.

Cinderella had two ugly
stepsisters who were very
cruel to her.

They made Cinderella do
all the hard work.

The two ugly sisters were invited to the Prince's ball at the royal palace.

Cinderella wished that she could go too.

Suddenly, a fairy appeared.
"I'm your fairy godmother,"
she told Cinderella.

She waved her magic
wand ...

Cinderella's rags turned
into a beautiful dress.

On her feet were sparkling
glass slippers.

The fairy godmother turned a pumpkin into an amazing coach.

14

Then she turned some
mice into horses.

"Have fun," she said to Cinderella, "but be back by midnight or else!"

"Thank you!" cried Cinderella.

At the ball, everyone wondered who the beautiful princess was.

The Prince danced every dance with her.

When the clock began to strike twelve, Cinderella suddenly remembered.

She ran back to the coach
but lost one of her glass
slippers on the way.

Then the coach and
horses disappeared.

Cinderella's beautiful dress turned back to rags.

The next day the Prince set
out to find Cinderella again.

Every girl in the kingdom
tried on the glass slipper ...

... but it didn't fit.

The ugly sisters tried to fit into the slipper but their feet were much too big.

"Let this girl try," said the Prince when he saw Cinderella.

"But that's only Cinderella," cried the ugly sisters, "the slipper won't fit her!"

But it did!

So the Prince found his
Princess and they lived
happily ever after.

Leapfrog has been specially designed to fit the requirements of the National Literacy Strategy. It offers real books for beginning readers by top authors and illustrators.

There are 25 Leapfrog stories to choose from: